8/12

W9-BWH-493

DISCARD

Put Beginning Readers on the Right Track with
ALL ABOARD READING™

The All Aboard Reading series is especially designed for beginning readers. Written by noted authors and illustrated in full color, these are books that children really want to read—books to excite their imagination, expand their interests, make them laugh, and support their feelings. With fiction and nonfiction stories that are high interest and curriculum-related, All Aboard Reading books offer something for every young reader. And with four different reading levels, the All Aboard Reading series lets you choose which books are most appropriate for your children and their growing abilities.

Picture Readers
Picture Readers have super-simple texts, with many nouns appearing as rebus pictures. At the end of each book are 24 flash cards—on one side is a rebus picture; on the other side is the written-out word.

Station Stop 1
Station Stop 1 books are best for children who have just begun to read. Simple words and big type make these early reading experiences more comfortable. Picture clues help children to figure out the words on the page. Lots of repetition throughout the text helps children to predict the next word or phrase—an essential step in developing word recognition.

Station Stop 2
Station Stop 2 books are written specifically for children who are reading with help. Short sentences make it easier for early readers to understand what they are reading. Simple plots and simple dialogue help children with reading comprehension.

Station Stop 3
Station Stop 3 books are perfect for children who are reading alone. With longer text and harder words, these books appeal to children who have mastered basic reading skills. More complex stories captivate children who are ready for more challenging books.

In addition to All Aboard Reading books, look for All Aboard Math Readers™ (fiction stories that teach math concepts children are learning in school); All Aboard Science Readers™ (nonfiction books that explore the most fascinating science topics in age-appropriate language); All Aboard Poetry Readers™ (funny, rhyming poems for readers of all levels); and All Aboard Mystery Readers™ (puzzling tales where children piece together evidence with the characters).

All Aboard for happy reading!

GROSSET & DUNLAP
Published by the Penguin Group
Penguin Group (USA) Inc., 375 Hudson Street,
New York, New York 10014, USA
Penguin Group (Canada), 90 Eglinton Avenue East, Suite 700,
Toronto, Ontario M4P 2Y3, Canada
(a division of Pearson Penguin Canada Inc.)
Penguin Books Ltd., 80 Strand, London WC2R 0RL, England
Penguin Group Ireland, 25 St. Stephen's Green, Dublin 2, Ireland
(a division of Penguin Books Ltd.)
Penguin Group (Australia), 250 Camberwell Road, Camberwell, Victoria 3124, Australia
(a division of Pearson Australia Group Pty. Ltd.)
Penguin Books India Pvt. Ltd., 11 Community Centre,
Panchsheel Park, New Delhi—110 017, India
Penguin Group (NZ), 67 Apollo Drive, Rosedale, North Shore 0632, New Zealand
(a division of Pearson New Zealand Ltd.)
Penguin Books (South Africa) (Pty.) Ltd., 24 Sturdee Avenue,
Rosebank, Johannesburg 2196, South Africa

Penguin Books Ltd., Registered Offices:
80 Strand, London WC2R 0RL, England

The scanning, uploading, and distribution of this book via the Internet or via any other
means without the permission of the publisher is illegal and punishable by law. Please purchase only authorized
electronic editions and do not participate in or encourage electronic piracy of copyrighted materials.
Your support of the author's rights is appreciated.

Based upon the animated series Max & Ruby
A Nelvana Limited production © 2002–2003.

Max & Ruby™ and © Rosemary Wells. Licensed by Nelvana Limited NELVANA™ Nelvana Limited. CORUS™
Corus Entertainment Inc. All Rights Reserved. Used under license by Penguin Young Readers Group.
Published in 2011 by Grosset & Dunlap, a division of Penguin Young Readers Group,
345 Hudson Street, New York, New York 10014. GROSSET & DUNLAP is a trademark of Penguin Group (USA) Inc.
Printed in the U.S.A.

ISBN 978-0-448-45593-8   10 9 8 7 6 5 4 3 2

Max & Ruby™

Beach
Day!

3 1389 02114 3920

Grosset & Dunlap
An Imprint of Penguin Group (USA) Inc.

Max and Ruby

are at the beach.

Grandma is there, too.

Ruby wants to build
a sand castle.

Max helps.
He digs in the sand
with his truck.

Max is hot.

He wants to swim.

Ruby says he
can swim later.

Ruby puts sand
in a bucket.

Then she turns
the bucket over.
That is how
to make a tower.

Now Ruby needs shells.

She gives Max a bucket.

Max takes the bucket.

He looks for shells.

Max goes in the water
with Grandma.

Max does not find shells.

He finds seaweed
and a feather.

Yuck!

Ruby does not like
what Max brought.

Wait!

The seaweed looks

like grass.

The feather

looks like a flag.

Good job, Max.

There is more work to do.
The sand castle needs
a bridge.

But Max wants

to cool off

in the water.

Ruby tells Max

to look for a bridge.

Max looks in the water.

He finds some wood.

The bridge is perfect!

But the sand castle
still needs shells.

Ruby looks for shells
with Grandma.

Max keeps digging
in the sand.

Oh no!

The waves are getting big.

The waves will
ruin the castle.

But Max dug in the sand.

He made a moat.

The moat keeps the water
away from the castle.

The moat saved
the castle.
Way to go, Max!